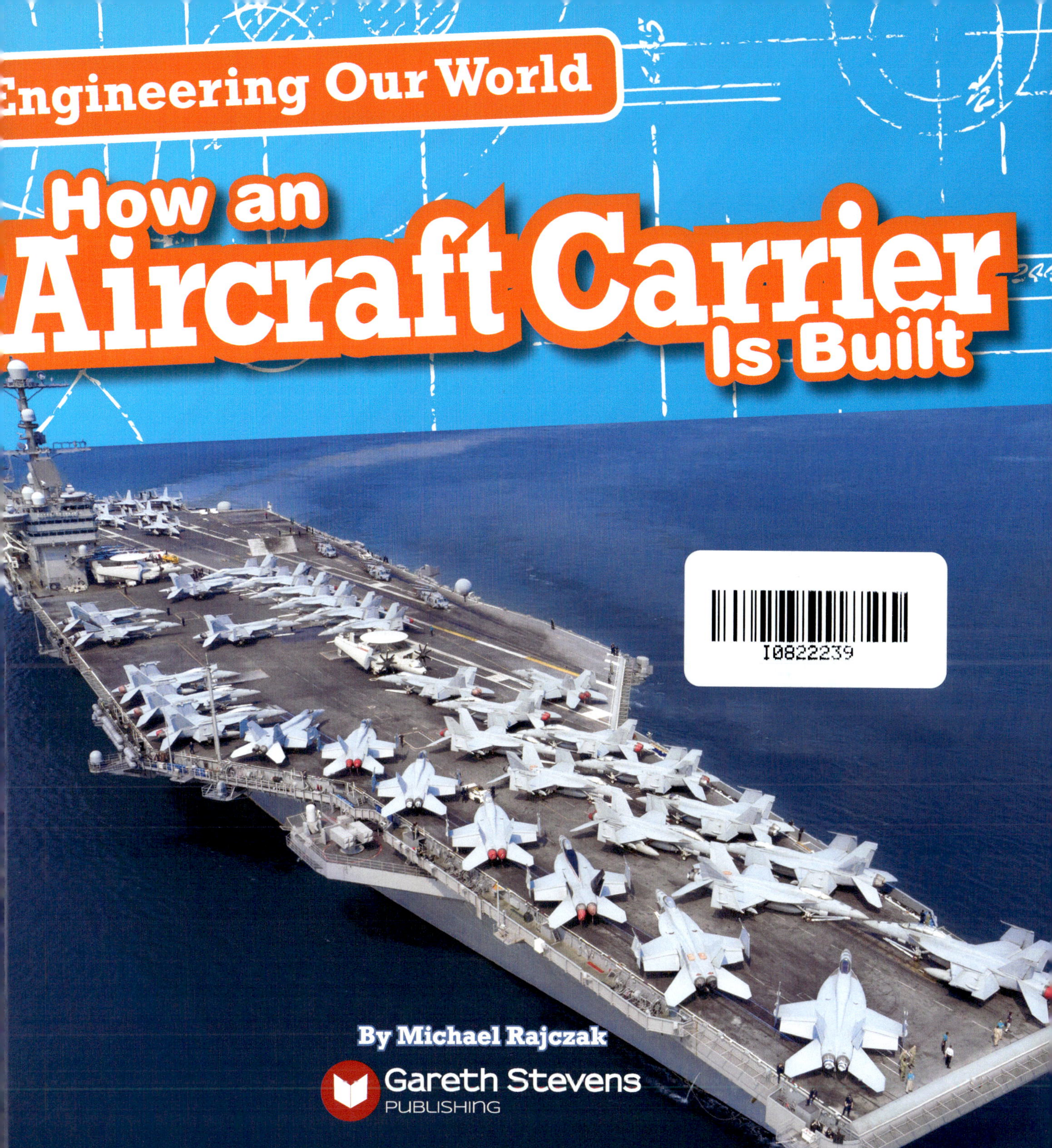

Engineering Our World
How an Aircraft Carrier Is Built
I0822239
By Michael Rajczak
Gareth Stevens
PUBLISHING

Please visit our website, www.garethstevens.com. For a free color catalog of all our high-quality books, call toll free 1-800-542-2595 or fax 1-877-542-2596.

Library of Congress Cataloging-in-Publication Data
Names: Rajczak, Michael, author.
Title: How to build an aircraft carrier / Michael Rajczak.
Description: New York : Gareth Stevens Publishing, [2021] | Series: Engineering our world | Includes index. | Contents: Building an aircraft carrier – The hull – Flight deck – Hangar deck – The island – Crewquarters – A city at sea – Powered to move – You can build a catapult.
Identifiers: LCCN 2019028941 | ISBN 9781538247198 (paperback) | ISBN 9781538247204 | ISBN 9781538247211 (library binding) | ISBN 9781538247228 (ebook)
Subjects: LCSH: Aircraft carriers–Design and construction–Juvenile literature. | CYAC: Aircraft carriers. | LCGFT: Instructional and educational works.
Classification: LCC V874 .R34 2020 | DDC 623.825/5–dc23
LC record available at https://lccn.loc.gov/2019028941

First Edition

Published in 2021 by
Gareth Stevens Publishing
111 East 14th Street, Suite 349
New York, NY 10003

Designer: Sarah Liddell
Editor: Monika Davies

Photo credits: Cover, p. 1 SUPHANAT KHUMSAP/Shutterstock.com; background Jason Winter/Shutterstock.com; p. 5 (main) Everett Historical/Shutterstock.com; pp. 5 (inset), 15 Matt Cardy/Stringer/Getty Images News/Getty Images; pp. 7, 19 FANTHOMME Hubert/Contributor/Paris Match Archive/Getty Images; p. 9 Avigator Fortuner/Shutterstock.com; p. 11 ERIC FEFERBERG/Staff/AFP/Getty Images; p. 13 Getty Images/Stringer/Getty Images News/Getty Images; p. 17 gmeland/Shutterstock.com; p. 20 (tape) Anton Starikov/Shutterstock.com; p. 20 (glue) Mega Pixel/Shutterstock.com; p. 20 (pencil) Vitaly Zorkin/Shutterstock.com; p. 20 (milk carton) posteriori/Shutterstock.com; p. 21 (cardboard) MichaelJayBerlin/Shutterstock.com; p. 21 (black paper) Marble background/Shutterstock.com; p. 21 Quang Ho/Shutterstock.com; p. 21 (crayon) Vangelis_Vassalakis/Shutterstock.com.

Printed in the United States of America

CPSIA compliance information: Batch #CS20GS: For further information contact Gareth Stevens, New York, New York at 1-800-542-2595.

Contents

Words in the glossary appear in **bold** type the first time they are used in the text.

Building an Aircraft Carrier

An aircraft carrier is a big ship with areas where airplanes can land and take off. It's like a floating airport that can move across oceans!

An aircraft carrier is made of very big sections, or pieces, called superlifts. Each superlift contains different rooms needed for the carrier to operate. The ship is like a giant puzzle, or something that has parts that fit together. When the superlifts are built, they are carefully connected together. It can take around 4 years and cost billions of dollars to build an aircraft carrier.

Building Blocks

Engineers, or people who use science and math to build better objects, work with **architects** to plan how the parts of the carrier will fit together. They use computer programs to design, or create the shape of, the ship.

CONSTRUCTION WORKERS USE A GIANT BRIDGE CRANE TO CONNECT THE CARRIER'S SUPERLIFTS TOGETHER. THE BRIDGE CRANE LIFTS AND LOWERS SUPERLIFTS IN A SHIPYARD.

The Hull

The hull is the base of an aircraft carrier. On its own, it would look like a long bowl or shell. The first piece put together to create the hull is the keel. The keel is built of strong iron and makes up the backbone, or bottom frame, of the hull.

Steel plates form the outside shell of the hull. These thick plates are welded together, or joined by heating, during the construction process. The greater part of the ship's wiring and **plumbing** is then put in place.

Building Blocks

Nearly 200 superlifts are needed to build an aircraft carrier! Each superlift is very heavy. Many US aircraft carriers weigh around 97,000 tons (88,000 mt).

THE HULL IS LONG AND OFTEN V-SHAPED AT THE FRONT SO IT CAN EASILY CUT THROUGH OCEAN WATER.

Flight Deck

The flight deck is the runway, or long strip, where airplanes land and take off from an aircraft carrier. This is the flat top of the ship.

In order to fly, a jet plane needs to reach a certain speed. Since aircraft carriers have such short runways, **catapults** are used to help planes get up to take-off speed. The catapults are attached to a bar near the front wheels of a plane. They often use steam **pressure** to then shoot the jet plane into the air.

Building Blocks

When jet planes land on an aircraft carrier, heavy steel cables attached to the flight deck are attached to a hook under the jet's tail. These cables absorb, or take in, energy to help the plane stop.

Hangar Bay

Located below the flight deck, the hangar bay is the storage area for jet planes and other aircraft. Aircraft carriers can carry over 60 planes! There isn't enough room on the flight deck for all these planes to sit, so they're placed in the hangar bay.

The hangar bay is nearly 700 feet (213 m) long and up to three decks high. Extra plane parts, gas, and other gear are also stored here. Giant elevators are used to move the jet planes to the flight deck.

Building Blocks

Aft, or behind, the hangar deck is an area where aircraft are tested and fixed. Jet planes land on aircraft carriers at very high speeds, so the jets need to be checked often for any damage, or harm.

THE HANGAR DECK'S ELEVATORS NEED TO BE STRONG ENOUGH TO LIFT JET PLANES. THERE ARE USUALLY FOUR HYDRAULIC ELEVATORS IN TOTAL. THESE ELEVATORS ARE MADE OF ALUMINUM, A LIGHT METAL THAT IS SILVER, AND MOVE AT HIGH SPEEDS.

The Island

A towering building nicknamed the "island" sits on the flight deck. It's often around 150 feet (46 m) tall. This is the control center and command bridge of the aircraft carrier.

Near the top of this building is the Primary Flight Control (Pri-Fly). This is where the ship's air boss directs air traffic, including all planes landing or taking off from the flight deck. A level below the Pri-Fly is the bridge. The bridge is where the captain and other commanding officers **navigate** and drive the ship.

Building Blocks

The control center receives a lot of data, or facts and figures, to help officers carry out their tasks. The data received includes weather and sea conditions, as well as **satellite** reports.

AT THE TOP OF THE CONTROL CENTER ARE MULTIPLE ANTENNAS, OR METAL RODS OR WIRES USED TO SEND AND RECEIVE RADIO WAVES. THE RADIO WAVES CAN LOCATE WHERE OTHER SHIPS ARE NEARBY.

Crew Quarters

There is limited space aboard an aircraft carrier. There can be over 5,000 people living and working on these ships. Crew members live in quarters that are compact, or very close together. This is where crew members sleep and have their personal space.

Most crew members stay in quarters with up to 60 other members, sleeping on single beds stacked up in sets of three. Down here, there aren't usually any windows. If you want to see sunlight, you have to get **permission** to go to the flight deck.

Building Blocks

An aircraft carrier also has several galleys, or kitchens, as well as mess halls. Mess halls are where crew members eat their meals. On a carrier, up to 18,000 meals could be served in a day!

THE SINGLE BUNKS IN CREW QUARTERS ARE OFTEN CALLED RACKS. AS YOU CAN SEE, SPACE IS VERY TIGHT ON AN AIRCRAFT CARRIER!

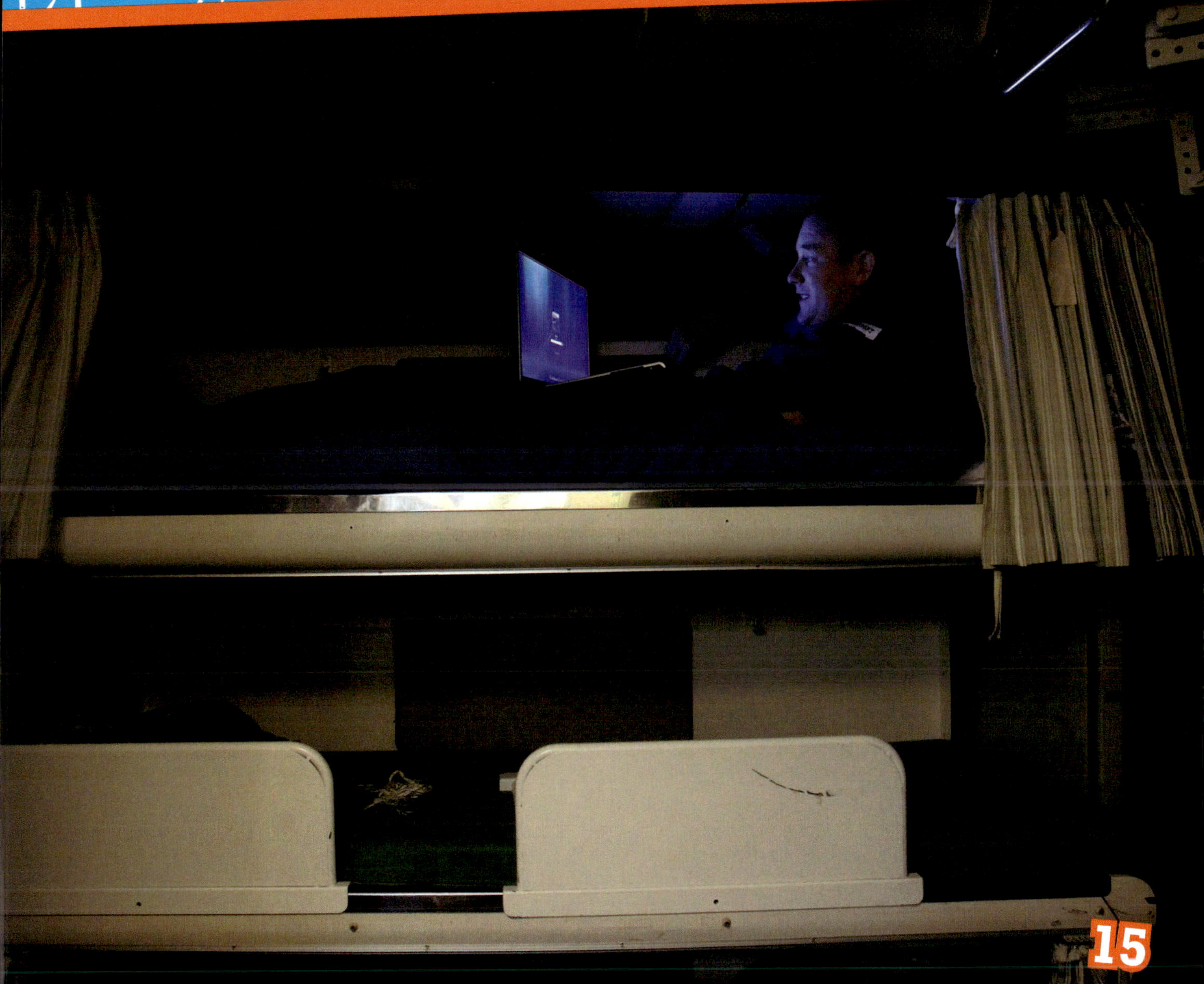

A City at Sea

An aircraft carrier is sometimes called a "city at sea." It's built to meet the needs of everyone onboard. You can find a dentist's office, gyms, and even a barber shop on an aircraft carrier. There are also rooms for resting with TVs, as well as a post office.

There can be a hospital on every ship, and a team of doctors and nurses treat illnesses here. Each of these areas are planned for and built before being added to the aircraft carrier.

Building Blocks

From the 1930s onward, nearly all US aircraft carriers have been put together in Newport News, Virginia.

AIRCRAFT CARRIERS CAN BE AS TALL AS A 24-STORY BUILDING AND THE STEEL USED TO BUILD THEM CAN WEIGH AS MUCH AS 60,000 TONS (54,400 MT).

Powered to Move

American aircraft carriers can use two nuclear reactors to create steam that powers the ship's engines. The huge **turbine engines** spin the large propellers at the back of the ship, moving the ship forward. The engines also create electricity that powers everything on board.

An aircraft carrier can move surprisingly fast for such a large ship. It can reach speeds of around 35 miles (56 km) per hour! Nuclear-powered aircraft carriers can travel for up to 20 years without having to stop and get more power.

Building Blocks

The **nuclei** in atoms are split in a nuclear reactor. Nuclear reactors must be put on ships very carefully.

PROPELLERS ARE PADDLE-LIKE PARTS ON A SHIP THAT SPIN IN THE WATER TO MOVE THE SHIP FORWARD. AN AIRCRAFT CARRIER'S PROPELLERS ARE ATTACHED, OR CONNECTED, TO THE SHIP BEFORE IT ENTERS THE WATER FOR THE FIRST TIME.

You Can Build an Aircraft Carrier

Now that you've learned what goes into building an aircraft carrier, you can make your own!

What You Need:

- cardboard or poster board
- empty half-gallon milk or juice carton
- scissors
- colored construction paper (black, gray, or white)
- clear tape
- ruler
- pencil
- glue
- white crayon
- 2 to 3 small boxes
- small plastic airplanes

How To Do It:

1. Start with the hull of your aircraft carrier. Wrap your empty carton with black, gray, or white construction paper. The pointed top of your carton is the front of your carrier.
2. Using a ruler and pencil, trace the shape of a flight deck on a piece of cardboard or poster board. Cut out the flight deck with your scissors.
3. Use black construction paper to cover your flight deck. Then, look at a picture of an aircraft carrier's flight deck, such as the one on page 9. Use your white crayon to draw lines that mark the deck's runway for planes landing or taking off.
4. Glue or tape your flight deck to top of your hull.
5. Stack and glue your small boxes together to create your ship's control tower. Glue the control tower to your flight deck.
6. Place your aircraft carrier in a bowl or sink filled with water. If you have plastic airplanes, you can now "land" your planes on your aircraft carrier!

Glossary

architect: a person who creates the plan for buildings

catapult: a system that uses steam pressure to power a machine that shoots an airplane into the air from an aircraft carrier

hydraulic: operated using the pressure of a liquid

navigate: to find one's way

nuclei: the plural form of the central part of an atom called the nucleus

permission: the ability to do something given by someone with more power or authority

plumbing: a group of pipes that moves water through a structure, or something built

pressure: a force that pushes on something else

satellite: an object that circles Earth in order to collect and send information or aid in communication

turbine engine: a machine that makes power using a part called a turbine with blades that spin

For More Information

Books

Loh-Hagan, Virginia. *Aircraft Carriers.* Ann Arbor, MI: Cherry Lake Publishing, 2017.

Nagelhout, Ryan. *Aircraft Carriers.* New York, NY: Gareth Stevens Publishing, 2015.

Ransom, Candice. *How Aircraft Carriers Work.* Minneapolis, MN: Lerner Publications, 2020.

Websites

The Aircraft Carrier
www.navy.mil/navydata/ships/carriers/carriers.asp
View photos of the US Navy's aircraft carriers and learn about their history.

World Aircraft Carrier Lists
www.hazegray.org/navhist/carriers
Have a look at pictures of different aircraft carriers throughout history.

World War II: Aircraft Carriers
www.ducksters.com/history/world_war_ii/aircraft_carriers_in_ww2.php
Learn more about aircraft carriers and their role in World War II.

Index